for Mum and Dad

Printed and bound in Belgium by Proost
for the publishers, Piccadilly Press Ltd,
5 Castle Road, London NW1 8PR

ISBNs: 1 85340 589 2 (hardback)
1 85340 594 9 (paperback)

1 3 5 7 9 10 8 6 4 2

Designed by Louise Millar
Cover designed by Judith Robertson

Set in Bembo 28pt

A catalogue record of this book is available from the British Library

Sally Chambers lives in Hayes, Kent. Since graduating from
the University of Brighton she has illustrated a number of children's books.
Piccadilly publish her other picture books, BARTY'S SCARF and BARTY'S KETCHUP CATASTROPHE:

BARTY'S SCARF
ISBN: 1 85340 501 9 (p/b)

BARTY'S KETCHUP CATASTROPHE
ISBN: 1 85340 484 5 (p/b)

Toffee
in trouble

Sally Chambers

Piccadilly Press • London

Tweet! Tweet! Tweet!
The birds are waking up.
Toffee wakes up too
and stretches.

It's very quiet.

Everyone's asleep.

But Toffee wants to play!

What's that noise in the bathroom?

Drip Drip Drip

It's just the tap.

What's that noise in the playroom?

Maybe someone else is awake.

Buzz Buzz Buzz

It's only a fly!

Toffee chases the fly . . .

through the door,

and down the stairs. But the fly buzzes off.

Then Toffee sees the newspaper.

Rustle!

Rustle!

Rustle!

Toffee always loves playing
with the newspaper.

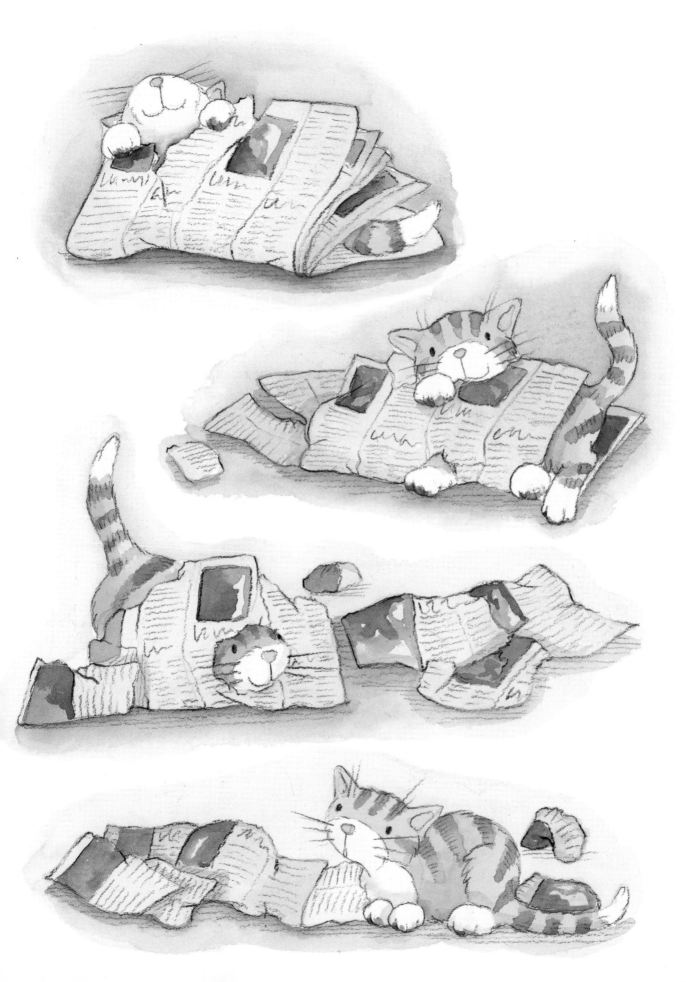

Tweet! Tweet! Tweet!
The birds are singing louder now.

Perhaps they will play with Toffee.

But all the birds fly away!

Crash! Bang!
Smash! Here comes Toffee, back again!

Now everyone is awake.
Oh dear! What an awful mess!

Where is that cat?
Toffee, you're in such trouble!

Oh . . . Toffee!